THE Baker's WIFE

The Baker's Wife
Copyright © Caytlyn Brooke
All rights reserved.

This book is a work of fiction. The characters, incidents, and dialogue are drawn from the author's imagination and are not to be construed as real. Any resemblance to actual events or persons, living or dead, is entirely coincidental.

First published by Kindle Direct Publishing 2023

First Edition
ISBN: 979-8-9877402-0-0 (Softcover)
ISBN: 979-8-9877402-1-7 (Ebook)

Visit Caytlyn Brooke's website:
http://caytlynbrooke.wixsite.com/booksbycaytlyn

Editor: Chelsea Cambeis
Cover Designer: Neil Hart

OTHER WORKS

Dark Flowers
Wired
Among the Hunted

THE
Baker's
WIFE

CONTENT WARNING

This book contains explicit sexual content including spanking, bloodplay, light BDSM, and choking. It also contains emotional and physical abuse. This book is intended for readers 18+ so please proceed with caution.

CONTENTS

For every reader searching to unlock
a hidden part of themselves.

"I licked it, so it's mine."
— Common Saying

CHAPTER ONE

"I need three teaspoons of baking soda," the baker ordered as he cracked three eggs into the bowl. It was the annual gingerbread baking contest tomorrow, and he needed to make enough to serve nearly one hundred guests.

The baker's wife fumbled with the measuring spoons, sending them skittering across the counter. A puff of errant flour ascended into the air. She hated working alongside her husband in the kitchen, and her nerves were frayed. He was an older bitter man, with a temper to rival that of the hot oven he abused daily in his quest to craft the perfect recipe. Today was no different, and the harsh insults he tossed her way only put her more on edge.

She clenched her left hand into a tight fist, obscuring two half-circle scars across the length of her palm. The new skin was shiny and red. The blisters had peeled off, but the flesh was still tender. She eyed the bright orange burner beneath the simmering pan, remembering the pain as her husband held her hand down until she screamed. The whole kitchen had reeked of burnt hair and charred skin. She'd cracked an egg and dropped a tiny bit of shell into the bowl— an unforgivable offense in her husband's eyes.

He also blamed her for the stench, which was why they were up at 3:30 in the morning baking the necessary gingerbread for the contest at the very last minute. It had taken forty hours for her husband to come out of his latest bender after the incident. Usually, she lived for those following days, when he'd apologize and be gentle and sweet, but with the contest looming ever closer, her typical window of reprieve had been passed over.

This time, once he woke from his stupor and declared the stench gone and the kitchen acceptable to work in again, he dragged her out of bed and slapped her face to jolt her from her dreams. Now, fifteen minutes later, she was standing in the kitchen with her forearms covered in flour, struggling to keep her eyes open. She gripped the end of the measuring utensil and scooped the proper amount of baking soda out of the jar before adding it to the dry ingredients.

"All set," the baker's wife whispered.

"Good. Now grab the rolling pin and cookie cutter while I mix this. We need to make dozens of these little men if I have any chance at beating Doubtmire this year."

The baker's wife nodded and wiped her hands on her apron, then retrieved the rolling pin from a drawer beneath the glass cutting board embedded in the countertop. She was careful to keep it tight in her hand, lest her husband found something dissatisfactory with the baking soda she'd added and had need of a weapon. Thankfully without remark, the baker began combining the ingredients, merging the wet and dry mixtures into one large bowl. His wife scurried around his bulbous frame to the corner of the kitchen where the baking cart stood. She let out a small sigh as she beheld a variety of tin cutters displayed in a worn woven basket that had been her mother's. Tracing her fingertip along delicate lambs, jolly bells, and proud reindeer, the memory of baking with her mother swelled and reminded her of the joy the kitchen had once yielded.

"Oy! Bring me that cutter, woman!"

The baker's sharp tongue chased the moment of comfort to the distant corners of the room far beneath the hatch to the outdoor window box. After locating the gingerbread man cookie cutter, she carried it back to the counter, where her husband waited with his arms crossed in front of his chest.

"Get your head out of the clouds. How am I supposed to bake if you're standing there mooning over your dead mother's trinkets?"

His wife hung her head. The past had taught her that every question he asked was a rhetorical one, and if she did try to defend herself, the sadistic bastard would reward her with a hard smack across the mouth. She ached for a divorce, but she had no money of her own and was terrified of what her husband might do if she tried to run.

It was 1907. After they wed, they moved away from Philadelphia out to a developing valley in rural Pennsylvania, enclosed by mountains on all sides. Her only hope to be free of him at this point would be for him to contract a terrible case of pneumonia and die before spring. But she had never been lucky. As soon as she turned eighteen, her father had started looking for suitors. Her mother had tried to convince him to let her stay, but in his eyes, she was a burden, just another mouth to feed.

Looking at her husband now, her stomach roiled with disgust. She was no great beauty, but surely there were other men who could have been interested in her. Instead, her father had agreed to the first man who asked, selling her off like a fat pig to market.

The one saving grace was that, because of her husband's long-standing affair with whiskey, he was rarely conscious long enough to touch her, let alone keep an erection for more than thirty seconds. Apart from their awful wedding night, he hadn't lain with her since. She frowned at the uncomfortable memory of when she'd lain sandwiched between his hairy belly and the hard mattress while he'd panted and grunted on top of her until he achieved a pitiful orgasm. She was grateful, especially that their union hadn't resulted in a child, but she was also lonely. She yearned to be touched in the way her mother's romance novels described, to be tenderly kissed and stroked, but sadly, that was a mere fantasy, a fantasy she was seldom able to indulge in because of the recent late-night baking fits her husband insisted she be a part of.

After she placed the cookie cutter in her husband's meaty hand, he directed her back to the cutting board. Sitting atop the thin layer of flour she'd sprinkled a few minutes prior was a huge mound of dough.

"Roll it out and cut out sixty-two gingerbread men. Arrange them evenly on the trays and bake each tray for ten minutes at 350 degrees."

Her eyes grew wide. "Shouldn't we wait to bake them? The dough must be wrapped and stored in the window box for several hours or—"

A hard slap rendered her speechless. Her left cheek stung, raw and painful, and she could feel this new assault deepening the already forming bruise from earlier.

"Thanks to your . . . accident the other day, we don't have time to chill it! Roll them out. After each tray comes out, you must let it cool before the next batch. Everything better be finished by the time I have to leave for the contest at eleven," the baker said, a warning look in his beady eyes.

"Where are you going?" she asked. Her eyes watered as a bright handprint bloomed across her face.

"To sleep. All the hard work is done. I need to be refreshed for the contest and all the prep work come morning. Don't drop a pan and wake me, or you'll be sleeping in the outhouse, understood?"

Biting her tongue, she nodded as her husband untied his apron and hung it on a nail in the doorframe. "Get to work." He growled and threw her mother's cutter against the wall, hard enough to crack the tin of his leg. The baker strode out of the warm kitchen as his wife ran over to cradle the broken gingerbread man in her hands. The right leg had come detached and now dangled inward. She allowed a single tear to fall after she heard their bedroom door slam shut. God, how she despised him. She glanced over at the mound of dough waiting for her. Already, it had started to expand, turning into a slime-like substance. She would have to work fast to keep it malleable and make her deadline.

As she set her mother's cutter down gently in the sink, her despair hardened to rage. To make sixty-two gingerbread men would take hours, even more now that her cookie cutter was damaged. She plunged her hands into the sticky dough, and soon, an idea began to take form.

If he wanted gingerbread men, she'd give him one he'd never forget.

CHAPTER TWO

Sun filtered in through the frosty window, kissing her eyelids open. The baker's wife rolled the kink in her neck—the result of falling asleep hunched over the counter. Her sweaty cheek stuck to the rolling pin with the last remnants of dough. The once sticky substance had hardened to crust and now adorned her cheekbone in spotty patches.

Beside her on the stove lay the largest gingerbread man she had even seen. Rather than dozens of little men, the baker's wife had worked all through the early hours to craft one massive gingerbread man. Using her mother's tin cutter as a reference, she'd molded and shaped the dough into an exact replica, only five times larger. He stretched from end to end on the silver tray while the dough rose just enough to be smooth, yet airy.

His arms and legs were nicely formed and proportioned—the perfect gingerbread man. However, last night, working by dim candlelight, the baker's wife didn't stop there. Once the gingerbread man was made, she'd cut off the excess pieces, and a handful of dough remained. She'd considered tossing the extra dough or making a treat for herself. But as she stood in the flickering light and bounced the greasy ball of dough in her palm, she'd envisioned her husband's face the next morning.

There was a split chance he would either be angry or elated at her bold choice to deviate from his instructions. After all, her mighty gingerbread would be unlike anything the judges had ever beheld. But then she'd shifted her jaw and felt the bruises that would linger through the New Year, and a devilish idea gripped her instead.

Rolling the extra dough between her hands, she'd shaped the spherical mass into a long cylinder before massaging one of the ends to an arrow-like point. Satisfied, she'd placed the dough between the gingerbread man's legs and took a step back to admire her workmanship. A half-crazed smile pulled at the corner of her lips.

Dangling between the gingerbread man's slightly turned-out knees was a long thick cock. Admittedly, the baker's wife hadn't seen many in real life for comparison, but there would be little else her husband could think it was. Her smile broadened as she popped her creation into the oven before she could change her mind. There was little doubt he would be furious with her, but it felt good to rebel. It was his own damn fault that he'd passed the responsibility of his contest entry onto her, and if he gave her a matching bruise on the other cheek, it would be worth seeing him be forced to touch the cock, even if it was made of cookie.

Yawning behind her hand, the baker's wife chuckled and admired the finished treat as she took it out of the oven. Once he cooled, she assembled the royal icing and piped beautiful curlicues and zigzags along the dark brown cookie. Incorporating white and black into the design, she brought the gingerbread man to life, etching roguish eyes and a mischievous smile onto his face.

He wore a snazzy pair of suspenders that ended mid-thigh with a necessary cut-out to accommodate his bulging cock. Using white icing, the baker's wife piped little veins and fashioned a realistic tip. When she was finished, she squirted some of the leftover icing onto her tongue and closed her eyes as she swallowed the sweetness.

This gingerbread man wasn't made to run. This gingerbread man was made to fuck.

Gently, she swiped her fingers down the length of his girth, giggling when she realized the icing had dried. It would be nearly impossible to scrape off now.

The thunder of footsteps echoed down the hall as the baker stumbled out of the bedroom. His wife glanced at the grandfather clock perched just above the threshold separating the kitchen from the living room. It was nearly 10:45 a.m. Unsurprisingly, her husband had slept until the last possible moment.

He blinked his bleary eyes against the bright light, but his expression hardened when they landed on his wife standing calm and collected in the kitchen, awaiting his arrival. "Well? Where are they? Didn't you finish?" His voice was deep and hoarse from several hours of non-use, and he cleared the phlegm from inside.

The baker's wife wrinkled her nose as he swallowed the wad of snot back down. She gestured to the stove where the decorated gingerbread man lay. The baker hiked up his drooping pants with the hook of his thumb and shuffled forward.

"What do you think?" his wife asked, her words an innocent song.

"What's that? Is that a . . ." His thick neck turned deep scarlet above his yellowed collar, and his jaw clenched.

His wife leaned closer. "What is it? Is something wrong?"

The baker raised a hand and extended his pointer finger, his eyes glued to the veiny cock staring back at him.

His wife grinned, her eyes crinkling at the corners. "You told me to make a gingerbread man. Well, I could think of no other way to emulate the ideal man but to bake one with a thick, long, throbbing co—"

"Don't!" The baker spun around, holding up both hands in front of him. "Please don't say it."

"Cock?" His wife tilted her head, an inquisitive bird playing with a worm. "But that's what men have, don't they? A big strong cock to bury in a woman's warm wet cu—"

The baker's eyes bulged before he spun away, hands pressed over his ears like a toddler throwing a tantrum. "Stop! Enough! Hold your tongue with that devil talk! I'm not feeling well. I think I'll head down to the pub and get an ale to settle my stomach."

His wife chased after him, gripping the sides of her flour-dusted skirts as she went. "But wait, you can't be ill. What about the contest? Aren't you going to enter your gingerbread man?"

"Enter that cookie with a behemoth of an appendage? What would people say? Absolutely not!"

"Wait! What if I break it off quickly and eat it? I could probably fit the whole thing in my mouth, and then once it melted a bit, I could swallow it easily," his wife called, trying to hide her grin.

The baker's strained face turned nearly purple, and for a moment, his wife thought he might faint. "What in God's name has come over you, woman? I'm going out. That monstrosity better be gone by the time I return."

The baker's wife leaned against the olive wing back chair as her husband practically ran out the front door, slamming it behind him so hard that it bounced in the lock and swung back open. She let out a hearty belly laugh—the first one since marrying the old walrus— and placed a hand on her chest. While she expected anger, maybe even wrath, she hadn't expected her husband to be so clearly flustered and flabbergasted by her depiction of the male reproductive organ and thinly veiled suggestion of oral sex. Perhaps that was why he had never tried to lay with her again. From what she could remember, his cock had been awfully small, barely extending past her opening.

She shut the front door and pivoted on her toes, untied her soiled apron, and let it slide from her hips onto the floor. Meandering toward the small washroom, she reached up and bent her neck to unbutton the clasps at the top of her dress. A relieved sigh slipped from her lips as the stiff fabric gave way, allowing her breasts to spill from their confined position.

"Maybe I should have made a gingerbread woman complete with a clitoris. I think his head might have exploded." The baker's wife laughed loud and carefree as she left the door to the washroom ajar—another first for her in this house. "Perhaps I can take a lover now that I know my dear husband is terrified of intimacy." Her voice carried through the small house as she shed the rest of her clothes and pumped in fresh water. "If only it were that easy." The baker's wife gathered the dry sponge and tossed it into the washtub.

Over the sound of falling water, she didn't hear the silver tray pop in the kitchen.

CHAPTER THREE

The baker's wife pressed the heavy sponge against the gentle dip at the base of her throat and closed her eyes as lukewarm rivulets of water trickled between her breasts. Soapy ringlets rippled across the surface of the small washtub, punctuated by her reddened knees. Ringing the misshapen sponge out, she smiled at the song each little droplet sung before it was swallowed up by the water below.

Too soon, the bath grew chilly, and her fingers and toes were a pruny sight. She stood and squeezed her thick hair from the base of her head to the ends, extracting the excess water clinging to the long blond strands. Then she hopped out of the tub and burrowed into a thin towel. The baker's wife hurriedly swiped the fabric over and across her skin, absorbing the water as it ran down her body. Once dry, she unwound the towel from her back, bent over, and gathered her tresses. Her breasts hung heavy as she wrapped the towel around her hair, the light pink peaks raised and hard now that she had exposed her body to the cold room.

Twisting the material around, the baker's wife situated the towel on top of her head and then glanced in the small mirror above the little sink. It was her mother-in-law's, old and tarnished with age with numerous gray blotches that refused to come clean when scrubbed in the bottom right corner.

She stared at her naked form, feeling a thrill of excitement when she remembered her husband wasn't home. Rarely did she appreciate her own body. The washroom was the only place they had hung a mirror, and her nakedness was unusually unnerving in case her husband passed by. He wasn't a sexual man, but it was easier to keep it that way with all her clothes on.

Her shoulders shook with a slight shiver, and her breasts swayed at the motion. Her bosom wasn't well endowed like many of the women in town, but as she brought her hands up to cup her breasts, their fullness fit snugly in her palms. Running the pads of her thumbs along the hard peaks, she circled them before giving each one a gentle pull. Her sex pulsed with need. She was tired of pleasuring herself all the time. She yearned for a skilled lover able to make her orgasm with a few talented licks or a volley of hard thrusts.

She grabbed her soiled clothes and pressed them to her stomach, then leaned out the doorway of the washroom. In all the excitement chasing her husband out of the house, she'd forgotten to bring a fresh dress in with her.

"Hello? Dear, are you home yet?"

The house's reply was silent, cementing her

confidence that she was still alone. Humming to herself, she meandered down the hallway. The baker's wife walked through the kitchen to reach their bedroom but stopped mid-stride. Something was wrong. She did a quick sweep of the room and inhaled sharply when she saw the silver tray. The anatomically correct gingerbread man was no longer there. Instead, only a few crumbs lingered on the shiny surface, with several more dotting the floor.

Fear made her teeth chatter and her skin flush with goose bumps. Had her husband come back and decided to enter the gingerbread man into the contest anyway? Or had he smashed it and threw it away? Peeking in the trash barrel, she didn't spy any sign of the gingerbread man. Careful not to raise her naked chest over the window ledge, she looked out into the garden, expecting to see the poor cookie mangled and crushed atop the grass, but only a sparrow sat there, looking back at her.

The baker's wife left her spot at the window and turned, continuing to the bedroom. She didn't care if the baker had destroyed the gingerbread man. It was a comical prank that would bring her joy for years to come when she thought of it. She also hoped it would provide a shift in their relationship, one in which he wouldn't be so quick to hit her anymore. The first step in taking back her power.

Stepping over the trail of crumbs, the baker's wife excused the missing gingerbread man from her mind, intent on enjoying the rest of her solitude, when a tall figure stepped out of the dark hallway. Startled, she jerked back and dropped her clothes as the towel slid from her head. Standing at least six feet tall, the man took another step, moving into the light cast from the window.

The baker's wife forgot her nakedness as she stared at the intruder. His head was bald, save for a wavy white line at the crown of his head that stood out against his dark brown skin. Piercing black eyes regarded her with amusement, the expression complemented by the crooked set of his smirk. Her cheeks burned with color as she realized he was naked too, his dark skin riddled with hard muscle.

"How did you—" Her unfinished question hung suspended between them as her eyes traveled lower. Stretching from his mid-shoulder to waist were thin swirls of white and black, intricate tattoos that resembled wisps of smoke across his flesh. For some reason, the art looked familiar. Lowering her gaze, the baker's wife put a hand to her mouth.

Hanging to just above his knees was the largest cock she had ever seen, complete with the emphasized veins and tip she herself had drizzled on just a couple hours ago. The baker's wife's eyes went wide as the man took another step closer, his gaze smoldering. She didn't understand why or how it had happened, but her farce of a gingerbread had come to life and was now standing in front of her, wearing the same mischievous smile she'd carved on his lips.

CHAPTER FOUR

"But you were—" The baker's wife twisted to point to the empty tray. "How?"

The gingerbread man strode forward, shoulders rolling like a stalking feline. "I suppose your rage and dark humor elicited a bit of Christmas magic." His voice was deep and husky, as if he'd inhaled smoke.

The baker's wife shook her head, trying to wrap her brain around the fact that her gingerbread man—the one she'd shaped from dough— was standing in her kitchen. "But that doesn't make any sense. How can you be alive if you were just a cookie?"

She crossed the warped wooden floorboards and stopped before the towering gingerbread man, then reached out, and traced her fingertips along his smooth skin. Unlike the gritty rough exterior she expected, his skin was soft and supple under her touch. Feeling both arms, her hands fluttered over his tattoos, marveling at the designs. She recalled piping the swirls and intricate loops. Lost in the impossibility of her creation coming to life, the baker's wife didn't realize how low her hands had explored.

"Keep going," the gingerbread said, stepping closer. "Your hands feel good. Both now and when you made me."

"You could feel that?" she asked.

The gingerbread man nodded and gripped her wrist, sliding it across his stomach. "More."

Biting her lower lip, the baker's wife complied, sliding her fingers along each individual muscle. As she touched him, she felt a warm pressure nudge her thigh. She glanced down, and heat rose to her cheeks as his cock pressed firmly against her.

"Oh Lord!" the baker's wife exclaimed when her own nakedness sparked to the forefront of her mind. She leaned back and moved to find her clothes, but the gingerbread man's arms came up, his long fingers grasping her full waist as his thumbs extended down to her exposed sex.

"Keep going," he rasped, voice full of need.

"What? No, I can't. I'm sorry. I got so caught up. I shouldn't have touched you."

"What's the matter? You touched it before."

The baker's wife opened her mouth to argue. Rolling dough was certainly not the same thing as stroking an erect cock, but he did have a point.

"Don't you want to touch that part of me too? Feel how hard you've made me?"

She closed her eyes. Surely, she was dreaming. Yes, she'd fallen asleep in the tub and had conjured this magnificent man.

The heat of his cock edged closer to the apex of her thighs. With startling clarity, she realized how wet she was. Her eyelids flickered open, and the gingerbread man was still there. His thumbs traced small circles below her waist, pulling her closer. Leaning down, he brought his lips level with her ear.

"Touch me."

Releasing a shaky breath, the baker's wife slid her hand down from where it rested on his abdomen. If this was a dream, she wasn't going to waste it. Her fingers bumped into the solid base a second later, and she let out a surprised gasp. She already knew his cock was long—she'd made it that way—but she hadn't realized how thick the real-life version was as well. Tracing its length with the tips of her fingers, she beheld his length, his girth.

His cock twitched under her light touch, and the tip edged closer to her tight center. The gingerbread man groaned deep in his throat, the sound a dark rumble. "You have no idea how good that feels."

"It does?" The baker's wife had never touched her husband like this. She'd simply lain there while he pushed into her. She smiled, loving the newfound sense of power she wielded over her gingerbread man.

"Take it in your hand now." His command was gentle, but still, being told how to pleasure him sent a thrill straight to her sex. Her thighs clenched together on their own accord.

Wrapping her hand around his rigid thickness, the baker's wife was astonished to discover her fingers couldn't fit around his girth. The gingerbread man dropped his head back and groaned.

"That's it, sugar. Pump it nice and slow."

She did as he instructed, marveling at the way the skin stretched and folded. He breathed deep, sighing at her touch. Encouraged, she pumped faster. A tiny squeak of delight fell from her lips when he squeezed his eyes shut and exhaled a harsh breath.

"Whoa, sugar. Slow down. I'm not ready to cum yet."

The baker's wife smiled and slowed her pace. "You're so warm."

"You did put me in the oven, after all," the gingerbread man replied with a wink.

"Oh, I guess I did." The baker's wife released a giggle before again becoming transfixed by his cock. She wondered what it would feel like to have that heat between her legs, deep inside her. She ran her thumb along the edge of his swollen tip. "Does that feel good?"

"See for yourself." He arched his brow and gestured with his chin toward the tip. Displayed at the end was a glistening silver drop. "Taste it, sugar. Taste what you did to me."

"Taste it?"

The gingerbread man's eyes burned in reply.

The baker's wife tapped the silver drop with the tip of her finger. The sticky substance pulled away in a thin strand. Raising it in front of her, she eyed her wet finger and then touched it to the end of her tongue. The heady flavor of vanilla alighted on her taste buds.

"Mm-hhm," she said, but the gingerbread man shook his head.

"Not like that, sugar. Get on your knees."

"Why?" she asked, afraid she'd done something wrong.

"I want you to enjoy the flavor to the fullest. Now, on your knees."

Applying gentle pressure to her waist, the gingerbread man guided her body down until her face was equal with his iced cock, then released her. She gazed up at him with wide innocent eyes, licking her lips nervously.

"Open your mouth."

The baker's wife complied, parting her lips slightly.

"Keep your eyes on me, sugar." Gripping his cock with one hand and holding the back of her head with the other, the gingerbread man took a small step forward and brushed the head of his cock across the baker's wife's lower lip. Circling up, he coated her pink mouth with a glistening trail.

"Lick your lips."

The baker's wife stuck out her tongue and licked her upper lip before sucking in the lower one. The vanilla flavor was even stronger and oh so sweet.

"That's precum, sugar. It means I want more."

A warm pulse shivered between her thighs. *He* wanted more? He was the most delicious thing she had ever tasted. She lowered her eyes to his giant cock. It was so hard.

Rising higher onto her knees, she licked the tip

again, hoping to discover more, but only the ghost of flavor remained. She tilted her head to gaze at him in question, and his eyes burned with desire.

"You have to work for it, sugar."

Her own desire deepened at the rumble in his voice. She slipped a hand between her legs. Warm heat radiated from her cunny and she dipped her middle finger into her center, not surprised to find she was slick with need.

The gingerbread man shook his head and reached down, pulling her hand away. "None of that, sugar. I want to be able to see you play with yourself."

"Promise?" The baker's wife grinned. She knew what he wanted because she wanted it too. Keeping her eyes locked on his, she parted her lips as wide as she could and took him in her mouth, nearly choking on his length.

"Yes," he hissed, grabbing her head harder and threading his fingers into her hair. "Just like that." Slowly, he pushed himself deeper into her mouth, the tip of his cock rubbing her tonsils. She gagged but then readjusted and moaned with need as he pulled her head closer, driving his cock farther and farther in. "That's a good girl. What a good fucking girl you are."

After pulling back a little, the baker's wife sucked hard, moving her head to match his rhythm. Adding her tongue, she stroked the underside of his shaft, first in quick little bursts and then slower, more languid licks. Then she pulled away entirely and kissed the head of his cock, circling the ridged tip with her lips.

Curious to see if she could take all of him, she gripped the base of his length in one hand and opened her mouth wider, then swallowed his warm cock until it brushed the back of her throat. The baker's wife choked on his girth, but the gingerbread man groaned and held her head in place.

"Fuck. That's it, sugarcane. Stroke my cock while I fuck those beautiful lips." He sighed. "I'm so close."

The baker's wife didn't understand what he meant, but she squeezed the base of his thick cock while he filled her mouth, then pulled back only to thrust farther in. A moan rumbled low in her throat as his satisfied exaltations rained down around her. This was the first time she'd ever had a cock in her mouth, and it excited her to hear how much he liked what she was doing.

His grip on her head tightened, and he swore under his breath. At first, she worried her teeth had hurt him, but then sweet warm frosting coated her tongue.

"Sorry, sugar. I couldn't help it. Your mouth felt so fucking good."

Swallowing the frosting, the baker's wife pursed her wet lips and sucked on his cock one last time, making sure she didn't miss a drop. A sigh fell from her lips as she withdrew her mouth from his softening cock. Using her thumb, she pushed the small droplet lingering at the corner of her mouth back onto her tongue.

She rose to her feet. "You taste amazing."

"You should know. You made the frosting yourself."

The baker's wife eyed his length, no longer stiff and ready. Arching an eyebrow, she squeezed her breasts, rubbing her nipples along his chest. "I hope you have a plan to satisfy me now."

Faster than she could draw a breath, the gingerbread man pushed two fingers into her velvet folds, his thumb resting on her clit, rubbing in smooth slow circles.

"Run, run, run. You learned how to suck. Now I'm going to teach you what it's like to fuck."

CHAPTER FIVE

The baker's wife moaned atop the gingerbread man's fingers, sinking lower onto her perch. "Before we start, you should know, I've only done this once. I don't think I'm very good."

Moving his fingers up and down inside of her, the gingerbread man threw back his head and chuckled. "I don't believe that for a second. You just made me cum with that magical mouth of yours. Imagine what that tight little cunny can do. By the way, what is your name? Your ass of a husband never uses it."

The baker's wife nodded as the gingerbread man increased the tempo of his stroke. It felt good—so good—to be touched by a man interested in giving her pleasure rather than finishing as quickly as he could.

"I doubt my husband even knows it. He didn't marry me for love, that's for sure. Why do you want to know? What will you do with my name once you have it?" She tilted her chin upward, her words a breathy moan, a challenge. Her anonymity was like armor, a shield to protect the most vulnerable parts of herself.

The gingerbread man didn't answer right away. Instead, he lowered his mouth to nibble on her earlobe, his warm tongue caressing the sensitive flesh. But the baker's wife wouldn't give in so easily. She held her ground and rose onto her tiptoes to escape his skillful fingers. The moment his hand slipped out, a feeling of emptiness washed over her. All she wanted to do was let him touch her again, but he'd started this game. If he really wanted to play, he needed to take a page out of his own book and work for it.

He cocked his head to the side. "Where are you going, sugar?" His words sounded more like a growl.

The baker's wife took several slow steps backward, a gazelle backing away from a hungry lion. Her heart beat faster as she envisioned what would happen next. She was eager for the chase, for him to hunt her down and restrain her, to press that heavy cock against her.

But not yet.

"Give me your name first, sir, and perhaps I'll tell you mine." Her smile was sweet, but the glint in her eyes spoke of more beneath the surface.

Prowling after her, the gingerbread man licked his lips and flexed the hand that had been inside her just seconds ago. He raised his fingers to his lips, put them in his mouth to the knuckle, and sucked. Lazily, his eyes closed as he savored her flavor before he removed them from his mouth. His lips made a quiet popping sound. "My name is Cyn, and your cake tastes fucking heavenly."

"Cyn, like cinnamon?"

"Something like that, sugar. Now, tell me your name."

The baker's wife shook her head. "I still don't know what you'll do with it."

Cyn stalked closer, stepping on the crumbs that littered the floor—his crumbs, once upon a time. His dark eyes roamed over her curves, lingering on her pert breasts for a long time before shifting to the smooth apex of her thighs. His stare was just as powerful as his touch. She wanted him, to take his length in her mouth again before climbing atop his thighs and bouncing up and down on that thick cock. But this was a dream, a beautiful fantasy, and she didn't want it to end yet.

"I need your name, sugar, so I can say it as I enter you, and split your folds with my cock until I can't go any deeper. I need to whisper your name while I pinch your nipples and slam your hips down onto my shaft, faster and faster. Then I'll flip you around, bend you over that counter, and thrust in and out of you until you cum around my cock and your sweet essence is dripping down my length. And then, when you're sated, I'll hold you close and sing your name as I kiss the swells of your breasts until you're ready for more."

The baker's wife's eyes widened, and her body pulsed again with fervent need. Everything he'd said sounded incredible, and her traitorous cunny dripped for his touch. Shifting her eyes away from his face, she noticed that his cock was hard once again, eager to make good on his promises. Bouncing on the balls of her feet, she spun around, showing him her ass for the first time. "Okay, but you'll have to catch me first."

CHAPTER SIX

The baker's wife raced through the narrow hallway into the living room. Cyn was close behind, growling low in his throat. She stood behind the olive wing back chair. There was a wild look in his eyes, like he wanted to claim her. Like he *intended* to claim her. He was the hunter, and she had never been more excited to be prey.

Faking left and then moving right, she snaked under his arm just seconds before he caught her. His forearm grazed her nipples as she ran past, and a delicious shiver seized her. After skirting the coffee table, she maneuvered past the end table that housed her husband's important papers and pen collection, her destination the parlor on the other side of the archway.

The baker's wife thought she had evaded the gingerbread man when a viselike grip caught her around the waist and pulled her against his lean frame. Her ass pushed his cock upward so that it rested against her back, and the heat from him did unimaginable things to her body. He was so close and so ready.

"Fun trick, sugarcane, but I'm done running. I want my prize."

Holding her arms behind her back, Cyn walked the baker's wife forward, jostling her against the wooden frame of the archway. Her cheek pressed into the wood.

"Give me your name, sugar."

"No," she said, the word muffled against the doorframe.

Cupping her sex in his palm, Cyn teased her opening, gently tapping her sensitive pearl. The baker's wife groaned, wanting more.

"Your name."

"It doesn't matter."

He applied more pressure, easing the tip of his finger between her folds. She winced, inhaling sharply through her teeth as she arched her back, trying to force his finger in deeper. Cyn laughed, careful to only push his finger in up to the first joint, knowing full well how unsatisfied it left her.

He leaned in closer, his breath tickling her ear. It smelled like warm peppermint. Was every part of this man edible? At the thought of sucking him again, she arched her back to rub her ass against the base of his cock.

He snickered. "Come on, sugar. You really don't want me to have to ask again. Tell me your name, or I won't put this cock in your pretty wet cunt. In fact, I'll stop touching you altogether."

As soon as the words left his lips, he stepped away from her, abandoning her where she stood pressed against the wall. Without thinking, she reached back and gripped his cock, pulling him back and pressing the tip between her cheeks so he could feel her wetness. Cyn took her by the throat, wrapping his large hand around the front of her neck while the other slid across her chest. His fingers held her right nipple hostage, but she didn't surrender her hold, determined to keep him in place.

"Is this where you want me?" Cyn asked, giving her neck a little squeeze. "Holding you like this?"

The baker's wife had never done anything like this before, but it was exactly what she wanted. Exactly how she wanted to be taken.

"Yes . . . Fuck me right here."

Cyn tsked and rolled her nipple between his thumb and pointer finger, teasing it until it hardened. Then he pulled, earning a small moan from her lips. "Do you like that, sugar?"

"Yes." She bounced on the balls of her feet, shaking her ass on the head of his cock.

He leaned back, applying more pressure to the spot she craved. Letting go of her nipple, Cyn palmed his cock and lifted it up, slipping it between her ass cheeks, tip facing the ceiling. Reaching behind, the baker's wife gripped her ass and spread it wide, loving the way it felt when he rubbed his shaft along her curves. Her hips rolled. She was obsessed with the heat of him.

She moaned. "I want you inside me."

Cyn yanked her back, tightening his grip on her neck. With her new posture, his cock came loose, taking the glorious heat along with it. He held her jaw and twisted her head to the left. Capturing her lips with his, he forced his tongue into her mouth while abusing her lower lip with his teeth. Then he rained hot kisses across her cheekbone and down her neck, where he bit hard enough to draw small gasps.

"Now, Cyn. Put your cock inside me." The baker's wife rolled her hips with more purpose, bucking against him.

"My name sounds so good in your mouth. Say it again."

"Fuck me, Cyn."

"Again."

"Cyn, fuck me hard."

"No, sugar. Not until you tell me your name."

The baker's wife groaned and wiggled, trying to find his cock with her body.

Cyn pulled away. "Your name." His grip on her tightened. She could feel the bruises beginning to form from his fingers, his hard kisses. He flipped her around, then stroked his cock, his hand tracing the veins she'd sketched on him. Faster, he stroked himself while he held her in place. Her breasts rose and fell, her breath coming out in pants. She rolled her hips once more, trying to place her slick opening on the tip of his cock. Cyn moaned, closing his eyes. "Your name, sugar. I can't last much longer, and I want to spill my seed in your tight little cunt."

The baker's wife opened her mouth, but her reply stuck in her throat. She knew she should just tell him. There would be little harm in sharing that piece of herself with him, but still, she hesitated. Her husband never used her name, and her parents only ever referred to her as "girl."

Cyn palmed the head of his cock, his thumb separating the tiny slit. He stroked his rigid length as his head dropped back in pleasure.

The baker's wife pursed her lips, eager to speak her name and trust him. "It's Em—"

But before she could finish the second syllable, Cyn moaned, his hand stroking even faster.

"Oh fuck. Fuck, sugar, I'm coming." Warm white cum exploded from the tip of his cock, dousing her stomach and the swells of her breasts with his sweet seed. "Yes. Oh, fuck. You look so fucking good decorated with my cum." He relaxed his hold on her neck and sighed, leaning forward while the heady scent of vanilla overwhelmed her. He nudged her forehead with his and planted a long kiss on her cheek. "You look so sexy right now."

The baker's wife blushed and glanced down at herself. Cum the color of whipped icing covered her body from her breasts to her navel. It was warm, melting down toward her cunny like frosting on a fresh baked cookie. She didn't answer right away. He'd held out on purpose because she wouldn't give him her name, but a part of her was still bitter. Cyn had gotten off twice now, and he had barely touched her. She had yet to receive one ounce of release. A slow smile pulled her lips to the side. Fine. If that was how he wanted to play...

"It's okay. I understand." The baker's wife shrugged. Lowering her head, she pushed her breast up to her mouth. She sucked the hard peak between her lips and extended her tongue to lick the icing-like cum. She closed her eyes and sighed. It tasted so good, like gooey marshmallow.

Cyn drew a sharp breath between his teeth as he watched. Pushing her breasts together, she turned her attention to her other nipple. Cum drizzled in a diagonal across her chest, and she lapped it up easily.

"What are you doing?" Cyn asked.

The baker's wife's eyes fluttered open. "What? I don't want to waste it."

Cyn exhaled shakily in front of her. "I know what you want. I want it too, but I can't rebound that fast. You should have told me your name."

She released her breast and Cyn's gaze followed the puckered nipple as it swayed back into place. She licked her lips. Glancing down, she saw what he meant. His once throbbing cock now hung loose between his thighs. He'd rallied quickly after the kitchen, but if he was done for the day, she'd have to find some other way to satisfy herself.

"It's okay. Really. I'm used to taking care of myself."

The baker's wife strode past Cyn. Inhaling his invigorating scent of warm cinnamon, she lay down on the Oriental rug in the middle of the room. Positioning herself on her back, she spread her knees and pressed her middle finger to her clit. She rubbed it slow at first and then increased her tempo. Cyn's sharp hiss pierced the quiet. She glanced back to where he leaned against the wall with his arms crossed, watching her touch herself.

The baker's wife slipped two fingers inside her molten center, keeping her thumb on her clit. She arched her spine and looked back at Cyn, his image upside down, and moaned. "My name is Emma." She pushed her fingers deeper inside.

CHAPTER SEVEN

Surprise alighted on the gingerbread man's face. "Emma? Emma."

The way he said her name sent tingles down her spine. She arched into her own touch, imagining it was his hand exploring her instead. Careful footsteps sounded behind her until Cyn's face hovered inches from her own. Before she could say anything, he pressed his lips to hers and thrust his tongue between her teeth, sighing.

Emma's lips parted, emitting a moan. Cyn's kiss deepened as he gripped her waist and spun her around so that her legs pointed toward him, her knees open and inviting. Settling down between her thighs, he kissed her one last time before shifting lower. Desperate for his hands, his mouth, she pushed her breasts out, hoping he'd capture one in his teeth, but her chest wasn't his destination.

Lying down between her legs, Cyn wove his arms under Emma's thighs and pulled her even lower until his face was perfectly level with her fingers and her wet core. With a wink, he buried his face into her sex and inhaled, his fingers gripping her outer thighs.

"Fuck, you smell divine, Emma." He raised his dark brown eyes to hers, desire flaring in them.

Her fingers pushed harder, circling her slit. Having him smell her most vulnerable part was so hot. She couldn't wait to see what else he would do.

Without another word, he lowered his head and opened his mouth, revealing his wide pink tongue. Without removing her hand, Cyn licked her slit, leaving delicious hot trails up and down her sex. Then he turned his head away and kissed the sensitive skin on her inner thigh, the tip of his tongue flicking out, teasing.

Emma arched her back and withdrew her hand. She'd had enough teasing; now she wanted the real thing. Growing up, sex had frightened her. The only thing she knew about sex was that it led to babies. She'd watched the way her mother struggled every day raising her and her four siblings. There were good days with lots of laughter, but there were also miserable, screaming fits of despair. By the time Emma was twelve, all the light had left her mother's once vibrant face, replaced with exhaustion and resentment. That wasn't the life Emma dreamed of for herself.

Once Emma outgrew the awkward gangly phase of adolescence and her breasts grew round and her waist thickened, many of the local boys took notice. They'd follow her around, tell her how beautiful she was, and croon about how much they adored her. She would indulge their attention, kissing them behind the schoolhouse and letting them fondle her breasts. Yet, the second she told them she wanted to wait, they'd laugh and leave, labeling her a tease. And she'd saved herself for what? An old man too large to even see his own cock? No. She was done being a man's plaything. This was her dream. Why shouldn't she take charge?

Wrapping her hands around Cyn's head, she pulled him closer, tighter, delighting in the wet slide of his tongue as it slid inside her, tasting, licking, sucking. On and on, he made love to her with his tongue, gathering more of her body in his arms so he could go deeper. Back and forth, he moved, playing with her clit, alternating between sucking and circling it in fast sweeps.

Emma moaned, feeling her orgasm begin to swell within her. She reached down and ran her hands along the hard muscles of his back. In and out, his tongue moved. She rolled her hips in time with his rhythm, bouncing on his face. Cyn licked faster, flicking her little pearl with a knowing glint in his eye.

Digging her nails into his back, Emma released a guttural sigh of pleasure. "I'm coming. Keep going. Fuck, right there."

Cyn didn't stop, didn't slow his relentless assault. Damn, he was good. Knew exactly what her body needed and plunged his tongue in once more. Emma's body bucked as her orgasm crested, sending waves of rolling pleasure through her limbs to her fingertips and curling her toes.

"Ah!" Emma exhaled, squeezing her thighs around

his head before letting her knees fall to the sides. "Damn, you're really good at that." Pushing herself onto her elbows, she looked down the length of her body. Cyn's cum still covered her torso, and her own stuck to her thighs and puddled on the carpet beneath her.

Cyn looked up and smiled, licking his lips. "Thanks for the chance to satisfy you."

Emma batted her lashes. "I hope it won't be the last."

As he climbed off the floor, Cyn scoffed and raised an eyebrow. "Definitely not. I plan to make you ride my cock all over this house."

Emma's hips rolled back at the thrill of pleasure that prospect sent through her. Cyn had just made her cum, and already, she craved more. "And if my husband returns before then?"

Cyn's eyes darkened. "He can watch, but I'm not running anywhere until you've had your fill of me."

Emma tilted her chin down, eyeing her gingerbread man with growing passion.

Until *you've* had your fill of *me*.

She loved how that sounded, loved that he was content giving her complete control.

"Should we get started?" Emma purred.

Cyn grinned but shook his head. "As much as I'd love to, I'm not quite ready. When you take this cock, I want it to be as hard and as thick as it can be. You deserve nothing less."

Again, Emma's body quivered with delight. Patience was a virtue after all. "Okay." She nodded and rose to her feet.

"Come on." Cyn offered her his hand and placed a soft kiss on her smooth skin. "Let's get you cleaned up."

CHAPTER EIGHT

Emma sat in a fresh washtub of water while Cyn crouched beside her and gently sponged her skin. The enchanting flame of a tallow candle danced on the counter, filling the small room with the cozy scent of lavender. They weren't talking, but the silence was wonderful, a peaceful respite after their high-energy morning.

After cupping her hands beneath the water, Emma raised her arms and splashed her face. She blinked a few wandering droplets from her lashes.

"Here, let me." Taking hold of her chin with a soft guiding touch, Cyn dabbed at her eyes with a plush washcloth.

Emma's eyelids fluttered open. "Thank you."

Cyn smiled, staring at her with a look that spoke of pure adoration. Her skin flushed at the intensity of his gaze, and she looked down, swirling the soapy water with a brush of her fingertips. It was silly that she should find herself embarrassed. After all, she knew how the ridges of his cock felt pressed against the roof of her mouth and how he tilted his head back the second before he came. But while they were well versed in each other's bodies, she didn't have any idea who he was beneath the icing or if the magic that had brought him to life had also manifested a personality to complement the muscles and vigor.

"How did you get here?" Emma asked, flicking a small spray of water in his direction to diffuse the thickening chemistry. "At first, I thought you were a dream, but I would have woken up by now, and your mouth felt way too good to be conjured by my imagination. I've never done any of this before . . . I'd never have been able to come up with that on my own."

Cyn chuckled. "You should have seen your face when I asked you to put my cock in your mouth. You were so innocent to all of this."

Emma stuck out her tongue. "Let me finish."

He put up his hands and sat back with a grin.

"You mentioned earlier that you could remember when I formed you out of dough, but I've watched my husband bake hundreds of gingerbread men before. You're the first to come alive."

Turning the washcloth on himself, Cyn dried the clinging drops from his cheek and shrugged. "Truthfully, I have no idea what happened. I don't know what makes me special compared to all the rest, but I think it has something to do with you."

"Me?" Emma wrinkled her nose. "But I barely did anything. My husband made the dough, same as always."

Cyn nodded. "But it was your decision to create me, right? As you sculpted my head, my arms, my"—he gestured to the large adornment most gingerbread men went without— "you gave me life, my personality. You put every ounce of raw emotion into rolling me out. Somehow, between the oven and decorating, every detail you added made me more real. As you iced me, I could feel every swirl, every curve you created, along with all your heartbreak, disappointment, and passion for a life far different than the one you've found yourself in."

Cyn worried the washcloth between his large hands. "I wanted to be a gingerbread man you could be proud of. Though your husband's reaction was so volatile . . ."

Emma chuckled, remembering the terrified look on her husband's face. "You scared him."

Cyn lowered his brows. "How?"

Reaching over the wash barrel, Emma pointed down. "Your cock is far larger than his." She covered her mouth and giggled. "He couldn't face the truth that a cookie was more adequate than he'd ever be."

Threading his fingers through hers, Cyn pulled Emma's hand away from her face. "Don't ever cover your face when you laugh. Your joy is too pure to hide away."

Emma pinched her lips tightly together. "My mother told me I had an ugly laugh when I was younger. According to her, classy ladies laugh discreetly."

Cyn's eyebrows arched as he leaned forward to prop his elbows on the wooden sides of the washtub. "A classy lady, huh? Tell me then, how does a classy lady fuck?"

Emma smiled, eyes sparkling. "I can assure you, sir, that classy women never fuck. They make love."

"Then it's a damn good thing your laugh is too big and joyous to belong to a *lady*." His voice seemed to drop an octave, and the husky timbre soaked right into her core.

"My thoughts exactly." Emma matched his burning gaze and leaned forward. Cyn mirrored her movement, and when their lips were only a hair's breadth apart, she lifted her chin and licked his face, dragging her tongue from his lips to his forehead. His cinnamon flavor danced in her mouth.

Cyn playfully pushed her away. "Ah! Foul!"

Emma grinned and pressed her hands together, directing a line of water straight at his bare chest. Cyn was quick to splash her back with a wave of water. Emma cackled while trying to defend herself and then sighed as darker thoughts formed. "What's going to happen?"

"I'm going to dunk you under, that's what."

"No, I mean when my husband returns. Or when the magic that made you ends." Her face fell. "After this—after *you*—I can't go back to life with him the way it was before. I won't, especially now that I know what I'd be missing."

Cyn's lips parted as if he were about to answer, but he sighed instead, a heavy exhale that seemed to express the same uncertainty she felt. "Your guess is as good as mine. This is my first time being alive."

"What? Really?" Emma had to stop her mouth from springing open. "How did you know how to do all that stuff with me? To me?"

He shrugged. "The image of what to do just popped into my head, like reading an instruction manual. Like I said, when you made me, you poured all your hope and desire to find a lover into my dough. The moment I saw you, it was like there was a voice in the back of my head telling me what to do, what to say. And fuck, I couldn't believe how good you felt."

Emma grinned, sawing her bottom lip between her teeth. "Then we shouldn't waste the time we have left." Cyn growled and pulled her to her feet. After draping a towel around her shoulders, he swooped his arms beneath the backs of her knees and cradled her weight to his chest before turning and exiting through the door. As he maneuvered the narrow hall, he licked a stray droplet of water running down her shoulder.

"I want to lick you dry," Cyn said, his warm mouth covering the thin trail across her skin.

Emma laughed. "I don't think that's going to work."

Cyn wriggled his brow. "That's the idea. I love the thought of you wet and that I made you that way."

He stepped over her forgotten clothes in the kitchen on his way to the bedroom. Cyn set her down on the middle of the bed, then lay down beside her. Emma's hair fanned out in damp tendrils, and the towel around her loosened. Tracing his fingers over the exposed swell of her breast, Cyn pulled the fabric away, revealing one of her rosy peaks. Lowering his head, he opened his mouth, about to encase her with his eager warmth.

"Stop," Emma said. She rolled out from under him, cinched the towel tighter, and smiled. "I have something I want to show you."

Cyn groaned, moving his hand down to pump his cock. "Sorry, sugar, but if it's anything besides your perky tits or wet cunny, I'm not interested." He said it playfully, but desire turned his brown eyes black with need.

Still on the bed, Emma balanced on her knees, arms crossed securely in front. "I promise it'll be worth the wait."

Grimacing, Cyn dropped his cock and put his hands in the air—a silent surrender. Emma's gaze followed as it bounced off the quilt, the tip already glistening with delicious precum. Unable to help herself, she leaned down and licked the dripping icing, purring in the back of her throat when it touched her tongue.

"Fuck, Emma."

Cyn's fingers tangled in her hair, pushing her mouth back down to swallow his length, but she shook her head and leaned away. Cyn groaned, his cock twitching.

Emma climbed off the bed. She wanted to take him in her mouth and suck his cock while he thrust deep into the back of her throat, but if she did that, she wouldn't be able to stop, and she was running out of time. Glancing at the wall-mounted clock, she frowned. It was already three in the afternoon. She had no idea how much longer the tavern would continue serving her husband and his voracious thirst.

"Go on. Get out. I told you I have something to show you." Emma waved Cyn and his throbbing cock toward the door, careful not to look down. If she saw the way he yearned for her, she wasn't sure she'd be able to resist long enough to show him her surprise.

"How about I just stay here and close my eyes?"

"No!"

"I promise I won't peek . . . much."

Emma came around the edge of the bed and pushed Cyn to his feet. He moved a few steps, but then stopped, his body a solid wall of immovable muscle. He gazed down at her, dark eyes on fire.

"And if I don't? In two seconds, I could rip that towel off your body and have you pressed against that wall with your cunt wrapped around my cock."

Emma inhaled a sharp breath, her sex pulsing at the image he painted. "I have no doubt, my big strong gingerbread man, but it'll be worth the wait. Just trust me." She leaned forward and captured his lips with hers. Heat and pressure slipped beneath her towel as his cock sought out her slit, the head rubbing against her.

"Stop!" Emma yelled, smacking his arm with an eager squeal. "Come on."

"I'm trying," Cyn said, wrapping his hand around the back of her neck to secure her lips once more. Grinding against him, Emma opened her legs, her sex begging to be filled.

"Please," Emma whispered, but at this point, she

wasn't even sure what she was asking for.

Cyn's tongue tangled with hers once more before he pulled back. "Fine," he grumbled under his breath. "I'll give you two minutes, and then I'm throwing this door open and fucking you until you scream my name."

"Deal," Emma answered breathlessly.

With one last look over his shoulder, Cyn left the bedroom and closed the door. Releasing a desperate sigh, Emma let the towel fall and slipped two fingers along her opening. Wetness clung to her fingers. She was just as eager as Cyn, but this would be the only time she would ever have a chance to wear it.

Emma dug through the modest dresses and floor-length petticoats in her dresser drawer. At the very back, she felt the fine lace she was searching for. Pressing her thick skirts down, she gently eased the material out of its hiding place. Her best friend had given it to her as an engagement present. Unfortunately, that had been before they saw the groom.

Aware that she only had a minute left before Cyn came for her, Emma stepped into the white lingerie, doing her best to do up the hooks and adjust the straps. She looked down at her body and gasped at the see-through lace. The same swirls and patterns that adorned Cyn's arms and back decorated her flesh as well—a perfect match. She hoped he liked it. With only seconds to spare, she risked a quick glance in the mirror. Never had she worn any sort of lingerie before. She'd been so excited to try it on when Jane had given it to her, but that excitement evaporated the moment her father shared her future husband's photograph with her.

Unable to bring herself to burn the beautiful garment, Emma had buried it deep under her belongings to ensure her husband would never get the pleasure of viewing her in its delicate embrace. Cyn, on the other hand . . . She couldn't wait for him to drink her in.

The tight material pushed her breasts together and elevated them with hidden wire. Descending straps framed her backside, making it appear even more lush and full, and the clever cut-outs across her stomach whispered of the trove that lay beneath. Fluffing her damp hair behind her, Emma practiced a pout. A small wrinkle formed in the center of her forehead. Would Cyn think she looked sexy or ridiculous?

A slow rhythmic tap resounded on the door. She was about to find out.

CHAPTER NINE

"Knock, knock," Cyn called. He pushed open the door, then leaned against the doorframe, muscular arms bulging as he stood with them crossed in front of his chest.

Emma watched him sweep the room and his eyes alight on the corner in which she stood a moment later. She held her breath, wishing she'd thought to put on a pair of heels. Slinking to the bed, she crawled atop the coverlet and settled on her stomach. She bent her legs and pointed her toes, then ran her foot along her extended calf.

"Surprise."

Cyn remained where he was. At first, there had been amusement and wonder in his gaze, but it quickly darkened to an unreadable expression once he saw her. Emma cocked her head, her fingers worrying the ends of her hair. "Is everything all right?"

Cyn strode toward her then, shoulders rolling aggressively. He reached out, stopping just short of the bed. "Has he seen you in this?" His words were harsh, gravelly.

Twisting onto her side, Emma shook her head. "No, he doesn't even know it exists. It's only for you."

Something primal flashed in Cyn's eyes. "Good. Lie back down on your belly."

The command sent a shiver through her. Emma hastily complied with her arms in front of her, elbows touching. From the corner of her eye, she followed Cyn's movements and shuddered when he came closer. All she wanted him to do was touch her. She loved the weight of his gaze as it slid along her curves. He'd seen it all, had even tasted her molten center, but this felt different.

Before, he'd explored her body all at once, gripping, cupping, biting. Now he was taking his time, approaching with care, as if she were on display and forbidden to touch. Cyn reached out with his hand and ran his fingertips along the snippet of lace forming a small triangle over the top of her ass. The material thinned as it tapered down, and the gentle sweep of his knuckles mirrored the material, caressing her curves. Emma rolled her hips, arching her backside higher into the air. A stinging slap rang out, catching her off guard as Cyn's palm connected with her cheek.

"What was that?" Emma gasped, turning to look at him over her shoulder.

"Just a little reminder," Cyn answered, lips curling in a devilish grin. "You're dressed like an angel, but from the way your body's moving, I can practically hear all the devilish thoughts racing through your mind. Did you like it?"

He massaged the tender spot, rubbing and kneading her ass, his fingers edging dangerously close to her sex. Emma bit her lip. She'd never been spanked before—not in a sexual way—but she had to admit, she loved the thrill it gave her and the care Cyn administered after. Trying to be subtle, she shifted her weight and parted her knees. She stifled the moan climbing her throat, wishing his fingers would stretch just a little farther.

"I do," Emma said in her most husky voice. "What do you think of my outfit? Worth the wait?"

Cyn pursed his lips and slapped her other cheek, bringing a little yelp from her lips, but by then his hand was already soothing the spot, rubbing the stinging flesh. "It looks all right, but I'm not so sure. It looks flimsy, like it won't be able to withstand my onslaught." Bending down, Cyn planted warm kisses on her ass, lingering longer after each one.

Emma remembered the feel of his tongue dipping in and out of her on the living room rug. She arched her back again, pushing her ass closer to Cyn's mouth in a silent plea.

"Like this, for example. It looks so dainty, as if it'll snap. Rock back on your hands and knees, and I'll show you."

Before Emma could respond, Cyn climbed up on the bed behind her and gripped her hips, pulling her back toward him. His cock slid along her inner thigh, then grazed the soft skin of her stomach. Her cheeks flushed, and she clamped down to keep another moan from escaping. How deep would he go once he was inside her?

Letting go of her right hip, he traced the white lace from her lower back, between her ass, to directly above her slit. Emma bit her lip, glad he couldn't see her face. She knew she was wet; the material covering her sex was no doubt drenched. Rubbing two fingers up and down her sweet mound, Cyn sighed, adding just the slightest amount of pressure. Emma wanted to grab his hand and push his fingers between her folds, but she resisted, enjoying the tantalizing way he teased her. Sliding beneath the gauzy material, Cyn brushed his knuckles along her wetness, but he didn't enter her. Instead, he tugged the lace away from her cunny, then pulled until it was tight enough against her clit to cause pleasure but no release.

"Huh, sturdier than I thought," Cyn said, his voice betraying no hint of growing desire. But what his tone masked, his cock gave away. She smiled victoriously as he twitched against her opening. "What about the front, I wonder."

Faster than she would have thought possible, Cyn flipped Emma around so that she was seated on her knees before him, her light brown eyes as wide as a startled doe's. Gripping the material just below her navel, Cyn pinched it together in a narrow strip and began to tug, the lace rubbing her clit faster and faster. The material wove between her heat, eliciting a breathy moan from her lips. Without thought, she bounced, losing herself in the feeling.

Cyn sighed. "Fuck, sugar. Your tits look irresistible when you do that."

Emma threw back her head and pushed her heaving chest out further, begging him to grab them. Cyn growled. Using his other hand, he slipped his palm beneath the transparent lace, released her left breast, and squeezed. He bent his neck and captured the hardened peak in his mouth, flicking the sensitive nub with his tongue.

"Your gumdrops taste so fucking good."

Pushing the material off her other breast, Cyn directed his attention toward her other nipple, circling it with his tongue before nipping gently at the skin. Then he forced her onto her back with a firm palm. Emma moaned and grabbed his cock where it pressed against her thigh. Guiding it to her sex, she rubbed the head along her slit and then pushed it through the lace just the tiniest bit.

Cyn chuckled and gathered both of her wrists in one of his, then pinned them above her head. "Not yet, sugar. Not yet. Soon, I'll fill your lovely cunny with my cock, but I'm not done yet."

Emma's eyes widened. "What more are you going to do to me?"

"I want to make you as wet as possible. I want you dripping for me."

"I already am." Emma groaned and tried to wriggle out of his hold, but she only succeeded in shaking her breasts in his face.

Cyn smiled, dark and delicious. "Good girl. You have no idea how hot it is to watch you squirm beneath me. To smell your arousal." To prove this, he lowered his head and rubbed his nose and lips over the drenched lace. He inhaled deeply. The sound made Emma's thighs clench.

"Please," Emma begged.

Keeping her hands secure, Cyn nudged the lace aside and exhaled, covering her sex in his spicy breath.

"Lick me."

Cyn laughed softly. "I like you bossy." Ever so gently, his tongue explored her. Emma continued to writhe beneath him, rolling her hips and offering up her warm center. The pressure building within her was unlike anything she'd ever experienced. She needed release. She needed his cock pounding into her.

Without warning, Cyn's tongue plunged inside her, warm and wet and splendid. Then he licked her cunny from the bottom to the top, flicking the little pearl at the top mercilessly. Emma squeezed his head with her thighs, holding him in place while her body bucked.

"Yes, yes, yes! Keep going."

But Cyn withdrew his tongue, taking the sinful sensation away with him.

"No," Emma whined, trying to hold him to her, but he was too strong.

Cyn straightened and gripped his cock, guiding it to her opening at last. Emma moaned, thrumming with impatience. He rubbed the head of his cock along her exposed sex, gliding it through her wetness. Back and forth, he went. Keeping a firm hold, he dipped the tip in, just barely entering her. Again, she tried to slip her hands out of his hold, desperate to grab his hips and force him inside, but she couldn't break free.

"Fuck me, Cyn. Please fuck me."

Never had Emma felt such longing, such yearning, to be filled. What was he doing? Why was he torturing her?

In response, Cyn withdrew his cock and moved up her body so he was perched over her chest. Stroking his cock, he drizzled a small amount of precum onto her tits. The silver icing dripped between the valley of her breasts and the sweet scent made her dizzy. He leaned down and beat her breasts with his cock, thumping his heavy length against each nipple.

"Please, fuck me, Cyn. Please. I need you inside me." Emma's eyes rolled into the back of her head. The pressure was too much. She needed release, but with her hands tied and Cyn's stalling, she was going mad with longing.

"What do you want me to do?" Cyn asked, feigning confusion.

Emma slammed her head against the mattress. "Fuck me! Put that thick cock inside me right now!"

Cyn's smile faltered as he looked around the bedroom. "Is this where he took you? In this bed?"

"Yes, but what the hell does that matter?"

Cyn's voice dropped even lower. "It matters a great deal. I won't claim you where your coward of a husband has lain. No. We have a better place. Our place. That's where I'll make you mine."

"What are you talking about? Please, Cyn!" She arched into him again, but he was too quick.

Cyn rolled off the bed and pulled her to the edge. Gathering her in his arms, Cyn wrapped her legs around his waist, careful to keep an inch of space between his cock and her sex. Unable to help herself, Emma rolled her cunny against his abs, covering him in slippery kisses as she ached for more.

"Fuck, you're driving me crazy," Cyn said as he carried her across the threshold.

"So do something about it," Emma challenged, their gazes meeting at eye level.

As he crossed into the kitchen, Cyn's demeanor changed. While he seemed hesitant in the bedroom, confidence now radiated down the length of him. The kitchen was his domain, the first place they met. The perfect place for her gingerbread man to claim her and make her his. His hands gripped her thick thighs, establishing dominance once again.

"Oh, sugar, you shouldn't have said that."

CHAPTER TEN

A wicked gleam shone in his dark eyes. He pulled her hips away from his body. With her legs still wrapped around his lower back, Cyn drove her hips down and forced his glistening cock into her weeping folds, burying it to the hilt. There was no gentle easing, no hesitation.

A startled gasp was all Emma could utter as she clawed the top of Cyn's back, trying to hold on as he picked her up and slammed her back down, driving his cock in again and again. Each time, his thrusts seemed harder, as if he were trying to work out some inner demons within.

Guttural cries rained from Emma's throat, so raw and unrestrained that she barely recognized them as her own. Digging her nails into Cyn's flesh, she secured her hold and relaxed, trusting that he could support her weight, and she lost herself to the incredible feeling of fullness as he swelled inside her. Faster, he pumped. She gripped his length, swallowed his girth. Every thought fled her mind except for how good he made her feel.

Cyn groaned into her shoulder. "Fuck, sugar. I didn't expect you to be able to take all of me." He brushed his lips across her breasts and sucked on a nipple with the ferocity of a starving man. "Your little cunt is so fucking tight too, just right for my thick cock." He gripped her chin and claimed her mouth with his, his tongue enveloping hers as he slammed into her.

Emma moaned into his mouth. "I'm yours. Take all of me, every piece."

Cyn stopped thrusting, holding his cock inside her as he strode to the counter. A bag of flour sat beside the stove—part of the magic that had brought him to life. He raised her ass up, and his cock sprung free, covered in her white slickness. He groaned and set her down on the edge of the counter in front of him. "Normally, I'd make you clean me with your mouth, but I don't want to cum on your tongue this time. This time, I'm going to claim you properly and fill you with my seed so my scent never leaves you."

Emma gazed up at him, tapping her clit, disliking the hollowness he'd left her with. She cocked her head to the side, her blond hair falling in waves down her chest, covering her breasts and the bright red spots where he'd bitten her, marking her as his. "What are you waiting for?"

With one hand, Cyn gathered her hair in his fist and yanked her head back to reveal her tits once more. "First of all, never cover these again in my presence. And second . . ."

Using his other hand, Cyn trailed his fingertips

down her body, pausing at the wrinkled lace that had slipped back into place without his cock to force it to the side. Hooking his pointer and middle finger around the material, he twisted his wrist, applying just enough pressure to rip the delicate fabric from end to end. With the motion, his knuckles parted Emma's folds, and she gave a moaning gasp as she started to move back and forth, grinding on his fist.

"Fuck," Emma said, closing her eyes. The ridges of his knuckles felt glorious on her sex, especially when she slowed her rhythm and pressed down harder, riding each hill one at a time.

With her lingerie torn, there was nothing between them. Cyn bent and massaged her sensitive bud with his tongue. Emma's arms shot out to grip the edge of the counter. Her elbow knocked into the flour, and its white contents spilled across the surface and puffed into a cloud.

Straightening, Cyn groaned and bit her lower lip, teasing it between his teeth. "As much as I'm enjoying this slow rapture, I can't take it." Flexing his hand, he eased his knuckles from between her legs and fanned his fingers across her waist.

"What do you mean?" Emma asked. She craved his cock, wanted him to slam back into her and make her cum all over him.

Cyn grinned, his lips pulling up at the corner. "I'm the gingerbread man, remember? Run, run, run as fast as you can? But hold on, baby, because I'm going to *fuck* you as hard as *I* can. Once I start, I won't be able to stop. Do you understand? You have to want this, me, the only way I know how."

"Yes. I want it all, all of you, as hard and as fast as you can," Emma agreed, nodding her head furiously. Spreading her legs, she waited for him to pull her onto his cock like before, but instead, Cyn took her off the counter and set her feet on the ground. With animal-like ferocity, he whipped her body around and slipped his foot on the outside of hers to push her feet together.

"Bend over." Cyn's voice was hoarse with need as he issued the command and pushed her facedown on the countertop.

Soft flour pillowed Emma's cheek, but she didn't care. Behind her, Cyn planted his feet. With one hand, he held her in position, while the other pumped his cock.

"I can't begin to describe how sexy you look with your cunt bared, so eager to take me." Cyn spit into his palm, then rubbed the head of his cock, spreading the saliva over his length. Emma scoffed at the unnecessary display. She'd been wet since the first moment he touched her. She welcomed him back, her slit giving his cock sloppy kisses. She was too horny to be embarrassed. She would never tire of him, of the heat that radiated from him like a working oven.

After lining up his cock, Cyn released his shaft and gripped her waist with two hands as he plunged into her wet warmth. Greedily, she swallowed his girth again, squeezing his shaft with an urgency she didn't know she possessed.

"Shit." Cyn sighed, beginning to thrust hard. Very hard.

Emma yelped, the pleasure and speed almost too much. Lifting her heels, she bounced on his cock, her ass jiggling, begging to be spanked. Almost in sync with her thoughts, Cyn slapped her right cheek.

"Do you like that, sugar? Do you fucking like it when I spank you?"

"Yes!" Emma cried, bouncing faster, matching his rhythm. "Hit me harder." Another satisfying smack echoed. "Harder."

She was surprised those words fell from her lips. For a moment, her husband's face leapt to the forefront of her mind as she envisioned his hand punishing her. She detested him and the casual way he hit her, a constant reminder that she was his. Not to love, but to abuse. But with Cyn, being slapped wasn't a punishment, it was a reward. A glorious reward that sent her spiraling into a pool of ecstasy with every stinging cuff.

"Stay with me, sugarcane," Cyn ordered, somehow sensing her wandering thoughts. "Am I boring you?" A low hiss snaked between his teeth. He withdrew his cock to the tip and stopped his movement, waiting, torturing. Emma pushed back, but Cyn held her in place.

"No! I'm sorry," Emma said. "I'm not bored."

Cyn tsked. "I want your mind solely on me. Dizzy with the way my cock makes it hard for you to breathe. Got it?"

"Yes, yes. I promise. Please."

"I'm not sure I believe you, sugar."

He reached over and grabbed the handle of a large wooden spoon from a container filled to the brim with spatulas, whisks, and ladles. The curve of the spoon caught on the lip of the jar, sending the utensils skittering onto the floor. He managed to hold onto the spoon and promptly smacked it across her ass. Emma yelped, gripping the counter.

"Was that hard enough for you, sugar?"

Emma groaned. It hurt, but fuck did it make her sex pulse. "Again."

Cyn obliged, flicking his wrist and spanking her again. The wood made a popping sound as it connected with her flesh and left a large red welt behind. A spike of pleasure rolled through her body.

"Are you paying attention now?" he asked.

Tears slid from Emma's eyes. The pain was more intense than she'd imagined. "Yes." She tried not to let her voice waver.

He smacked her again across her tender flesh. "I'll kiss these later to make them feel better," Cyn said. "But I demand your focus." A hollow skittering resounded as he tossed the spoon behind him.

"I promise. I'm here. Please."

"Fuck, sugar, you're bleeding. I hit you too hard on that last one." Cyn started to pull out, but Emma reached back and grabbed his cock.

"Later," she said. "Fuck me first. Please, I need you to fuck me."

Cyn growled low in his throat. "That's my good

girl." Wrapping his knuckles in her hair, he dragged her to the threshold of the kitchen and living room and shoved her against the doorframe. "Hold on."

Emma complied and reached up to grip the wooden frame. Moving his hand from her hair to her neck, Cyn's fingers tightened, and with the other hand, he lifted her right leg up and toward him, twisting her torso, opening her hips and exposing her breasts. Emma pivoted on the ball of her foot like a ballerina to open for him. When he had her how he wanted her, he buried his cock deep in her tight center at last, thrusting with a savage need he had yet to unleash. Emma screamed, overwhelmed by the sensation. Her tits bobbed up and down from the force of his thrusts. Cyn leaned in, sucking and biting the nipple nearest him. The competing sensations were too much. Emma was so close. Her body clenched.

"Yes, Cyn!"

At the sound of a key in the front door, Emma's head whipped to the side. No, no, no. It couldn't be. Her husband couldn't be home, not now. She waited for Cyn to release her, to run and hide, but he continued fucking her as if she'd imagined the sound.

"Cyn, my husband. He's back. You have to hide."

Cyn squeezed her neck tighter, forcing her to look away from the door and back at him. Only at him. "He doesn't matter, do you understand? You're the only one who fucking matters, and I won't stop until you and your pretty cunny cum all over my cock. Come on, sugar, cum for me. Milk my cock."

Dropping her leg, Cyn directed them to the floor, bumping a nearby table on the way down. A decorative lamp wobbled on its feet and then crashed to the floor near Emma's head. Ceramic shards skated across the hardwood; one even bit into her palm as Cyn laid her down. Emma winced, pulling the wounded appendage close.

Cyn went to press the cut to his lips but paused when he saw the ugly burn. "Why didn't I see this before? What happened?"

"It's nothing," Emma said, trying to tug her hand back from him.

"When did this happen?" The embers in his eyes cooled to steel. "It was him. He hurt you." His gaze lifted to the door, where the key scratched at the lock like a hungry cat. Her drunkard of a husband couldn't get it in.

"A few days ago, but it's getting better."

Cyn raised an eyebrow. "Getting better? It never should have happened." With his focus still trained on the door, he spat, "I'll kill him for hurting you."

A flare of excitement bloomed in Emma's chest. Never had she encountered a man willing to protect her like this. Briefly, she allowed herself to imagine what life might be like without the baker and his cruelty. The idea brought a carefree smile to her face.

"I appreciate that, Cyn, but first, I want you to fuck me." Emma leaned up and whispered in his ear, before biting his lobe playfully: "Make him hear me."

In an instant, her gingerbread man's severe

countenance shifted. "Oh, you want him to hear you scream? Hear my name in your mouth as I make you cum?" Desire flared between them, and Emma moaned as he dragged his thick cock down the front of her slit. "Do you want me to bury my cock deep in your cunt?"

"Yes!" Emma cried.

"Say it," Cyn ordered. "Say you want my cock." Emma met his burning stare and licked her lips. "I want your cock, Cyn. Fill me and fuck me as hard as you can."

Climbing on top of her, Cyn pushed her knees wide, then drove his cock back inside her like a hammer pounding a stubborn nail. Emma forgot about the key, her bloody palm, her husband about to walk in on the gingerbread man bringing her to orgasm. She listened to Cyn's words, focused on nothing but the pleasure his cock wrought as he groaned, unable to prolong his orgasm any more than she could stave off hers.

Wrapping her legs around his torso, Emma interlocked her feet and pulled him in deeper, her pleasure cresting. Her back arched, and her eyes rolled into the back of her head.

"Together, Emma. Say my name as I make you cum."

"Cyn! Cyn! Yes! Fuck!" Emma screamed, giving into the delicious orgasm that raked her body. Her toes curled, and her fingers balled into fists as tiny shocks of pleasure rippled through her. She felt the moment her gingerbread man came and filled her with his icing-like seed. Just like his cock, his cum was molten, spreading bursts of heat through her center.

Breathing heavily, Emma moaned as another wave of pleasure washed over her. She squeezed her thighs, felt her sex pulse, and held his cock in place deep within her. "Cyn, that was incredible."

Emma's husband's voice rang out in reply: "I'm glad you enjoyed yourself, dear. I hope you enjoy this next part even more." His slurred speech echoed from the doorway, followed by the unmistakable racking of a shotgun.

CHAPTER ELEVEN

"Henry, no! Put the gun down." Emma turned her body, reaching for a nearby throw pillow to cover her breasts.

"Remove your dick from my wife, sir, so I can shoot you before strangling the tramp." The baker stumbled to the left, knocking over a brass coatrack that held his gray church blazer.

A cacophony of bangs and clangs erupted as the rack slammed and bobbed a few feet from where Cyn and Emma lay before coming to a rest on the uneven arms. Cyn leaned back, pulling his cock out of her with slow movements so as not to startle Henry's trigger finger. Emma let out a low moan, unable to stop herself.

Rage billowed in Henry's glassy eyes. "You welp of a whore!" he bellowed, pudgy jowls burning red. "How dare you make a cuckhold out of me!"

"Easy," Cyn said, holding his palms up in surrender. Carefully, he reached for the blazer and draped it across Emma's chest. He stood to his full height, positioning himself between the baker and his wife. His cock glistened with her wetness, but his expression could have been carved from stone. "You're not going to put a finger on her ever again."

Henry snickered. "Is that right, asshole? Who's holding the gun, eh? I have every right to shoot your trespassing ass."

Emma climbed to her feet and clung to Cyn's arm as she tucked herself into his side. "We'll go, Henry. You'll never see us again."

Henry grimaced, contorting his blotchy face into a deep scowl. His deep-set eyes roamed up and down his wife, over her tousled hair and flushed cheeks. Then he caught sight of the trail of white cum dripping down her thigh.

"Shut the hell up! You're not going anywhere. You're my wife by law."

"But I don't love you and I'm not your property. I won't be married to you any longer!"

Henry roared, gripping the barrel tighter, aiming it at Emma's head. "You have no voice in this house, bitch. You dare to stand there and defy your husband with another man's seed running from your cunt? Marriage isn't about love, it's about obedience, and I'm going to beat you till you get that through your whore head."

"Don't talk to her like that," Cyn said, his deep voice threatening. "I told you, you're not going to touch her ever again."

"Is that right, pretty boy?"

Cannon fire erupted as the shotgun exploded, catching Cyn in the left shoulder. Emma screamed, pressing her face against Cyn's back to avoid the blast. A pained moan fell from his lips as his stance wavered, but he managed to stay standing.

"Henry, stop it!" Tears streamed down Emma's face as she turned Cyn toward her to assess the damage, but no blood met her searching fingertips. Frowning, she ran her hands along his chest. Moving up from his pectoral, she gasped as the flesh gave way to hard cookie. The skin around the gaping wound was cracked and crumbling, leaving his left arm immobile, but he was alive.

Henry exhaled through gritted teeth. "What witchery is this, woman? Where'd a giant like him come from, anyway? He's not from town."

Thunder rumbled deep in Cyn's chest as he pushed Emma behind him once more, shielding her with his good side. "She made me, right here in your kitchen."

"Bullshit. What are you talking about?"

Emma prayed Cyn had a plan. Henry had one shot left. She was somewhat relieved there was no blood, but what if the next shot tore a hole through his chest, his head?

"Don't you remember? You told her to." Cyn's voice was dangerous—calm and simmering on the surface, but Emma saw the fury in his black eyes.

"What do you mean?" Henry asked, the butt of the gun sliding from the crook of his armpit.

"Run, run, run as fast as you can. You can't stop me. I'm your gingerbread man."

Before the last word left his mouth, Cyn raced

forward, his movements lightning quick, yet Emma felt as if she were watching in slow motion. Thrusting his palms beneath the gun, he pushed the barrel into the air.

Henry's hands slipped, and the gun fumbled to the floor. Cyn brought back his right fist and then slammed it into the baker's jaw, sending him staggering, limbs flailing. Cyn hit him again, this time aiming for his nose.

Bright red blood spurted from the askew angle as Henry's eyes widened in fear and fury.

"Your wife shouldn't be obedient. She should be worshipped for the goddess she is." Cyn lowered his fist. "A man who preys on the weak, who beats them into submission, is no man." He gestured to where Emma stood behind him. "You're a coward and she will no longer be your punching bag."

At Cyn's declaration, Henry leered past the gingerbread man's undamaged shoulder to glare at Emma. "Is that so, dear wife? I put a roof over your head, food in your belly, and taught you the skills to cook that you failed to learn during your miserable upbringing, yet one good fuck and you're going to leave with this bastard? Is that your plan?" Henry spat a sticky white glob of saliva on the floor at her feet. "Well, don't come crawling back to me when he up and leaves you for a new piece of ass. Look at him. You think a man like that can be satisfied by one woman? And he's not even a man at that!" A loud guffaw shook his round stomach.

Emma stepped up, gripping the blazer in tight fists. Raising her chin, she glared at him. Memories of the last year flickered through her mind—every insult, every backhanded smack, every excuse she'd conjured to explain away her newest bruise. She took a cleansing breath and exhaled all her fear and weakness. Never again would he subject her to his cruelty or overpower her voice. Cyn had opened her eyes to what love could and should be. Sharing yourself with another wasn't imprisonment, but a privilege, and she refused to go back to that life, waiting for the next fist to fall.

"He's more a man than you will ever be, Henry. I don't know where we'll go, but we will make our own happiness far, far away from you." Emma's words were a whip, lashing and curt. "We'll gather some clothes and be on our way." For the first time when addressing her husband, her voice didn't quiver. Strength radiated from every muscle, and her heart beat evenly. It felt as if the wire tethering her to him had been severed, and freedom ballooned within her.

Henry's face drooped, seemingly withered by her powerful display. His eyes flickered back to her when Cyn took her hand. His furious gaze made Emma's fingers burn, but she only squeezed Cyn's hand tighter. He no longer controlled her. She pulled gently on her gingerbread man's hand, leading him back to the bedroom. Soon, they would be free. Free to explore the world and make love under the stars.

"It seems I have no say in the matter." Henry grumbled, pushing his weight off the front door to close the distance between them. "As a show of good will, can I make you something to eat to send you on your way? Personally, I'm . . . starving."

Launching himself faster than Emma could believe, Henry dug his nails into the sides of Cyn's neck, wrenching him backward. He brought his mouth to Cyn's ear and exposed his teeth in a wicked grin. Savagely, the baker chomped Cyn's earlobe, and the flesh instantly transformed to gingerbread cookie.

"No!" Emma cried, her brain struggling to process the horror unfolding. She still clutched Cyn's hand, but Henry's surprise attack was evident in her gingerbread man's terrified eyes.

Henry continued to devour Cyn, biting giant pieces out of his neck and head and spitting them onto the floor with frightening speed. Cyn tried to fight the baker off, but his weight was too heavy to counter with his injuries.

"Henry! Stop it!" Emma's scream flooded the house, the force of it bursting the capillaries around her eyes. She leapt up and sunk her own teeth into her husband's hairy forearm, but her bite did nothing to stem his onslaught. Perhaps he was too drunk to feel the pain, or maybe his rage had blinded him to anything other than his mission.

Whirling around, Emma spied the shotgun a few feet away, the barrel lying parallel to the coffee table—the same one she lain before as Cyn teased her with his tongue, teaching her what true pleasure was before furthering her lessons all over the house.

How had everything changed so quickly?

Emma grabbed the cold metal barrel and jammed it into the crook of her shoulder. Taking aim, she leveled it at her husband's head—the part of him that was doing the most damage. Without another thought, she pulled the trigger. The recoil slammed into her shoulder and sent her flying backward. She caught the back of her head on the edge of the table. Groaning, Emma gritted her teeth through the blooming pain and tried to focus her eyes. The room was a blur of red and brown splashed against white walls.

At last, her vision cleared, and a sob racked her chest. Slouched against the front door, Henry sat immobile, the back of his skull blown out. Crumbled gingerbread fell from his open mouth, and bloody crumbs were scattered across his chin and shirt. Collapsed in front of him was Cyn, one arm draped over his head that obscured his face from view. Emma touched the tender spot on the back of her head and winced before she scuttled forward on her hands and knees. Blood soaked the floor, but she forged ahead, knees sliding through the carnage.

At last, she reached Cyn. She moved around to the opposite side of where Henry had flopped and lifted Cyn's head to cradle him in her lap. He was barely breathing, his hardened skin cool rather than warm with the familiar heat he usually brimmed with. Gently, Emma stroked his forehead.

"Can you hear me?" Emma whispered, tears filling her lower lids as she looked at his mangled body.

She couldn't understand how Henry had accomplished so much damage in so little time. Huge bites had whittled Cyn's neck nearly in half, while nearly a third of his head was covered in teeth marks and large gouges. Crumbs and sugar dust covered Cyn's chest, and his body shuddered as he struggled to breathe through his injuries.

"Emma." Cyn's labored response was a knife to her heart.

Emma stroked his gnawed cheek. "I'm so sorry. I'm so sorry he did this to you."

"It's all right." His words slurred into one messy syllable.

"Come on. I'll take you to the kitchen. Maybe I can fix you." Emma went to stand, but Cyn's fingers found her face. His trembling hand stopped her movements, and she resumed her position, holding him closer.

"Leave it. There's no—" Cyn wheezed, chest shaking. "There's no time. I just want to hold you and kiss you one last time."

Tears raced down Emma's cheeks to dot Cyn's dark brown skin with tiny puddles. His gaze swiveled until he found hers, and he offered up a warm smile.

"Promise . . . me that you'll never let anyone . . . hurt you again," Cyn said. "I'm sorry I won't be here . . . to see you thrive."

"Oh, Cyn," Emma cried. "I can't do this without you."

Cyn gave her hand one last squeeze and chuckled softly. "Of course you can, sugar. I'll always be with you.

In every recipe you . . . make. Take his place and create your own delicacies. You're going to be amazing."
Emma leaned down and pressed her lips to his. "I'll make you anew. I won't stop until I find a way to bring you back."

Cyn grinned around a shuddering breath. "I'd love to see you again, sugar. Until . . . then . . ." His words were overtaken by a pained sigh as the magic slipped away and his flesh solidified to firm gingerbread, then crumbled in a cascade of iced pieces on the floor.

A wretched sob tore free from Emma's throat as she pressed the broken pieces to her chest. She licked her lips, trying to clear them of her salty tears, only to find the taste of cinnamon on her tongue. It wasn't fair. He wasn't supposed to die. He wasn't supposed to leave her there alone.

Emma didn't know how long she sat on the floor covered in her husband's blood and brain matter, along with her lover's shattered parts. She couldn't wrap her mind around how suddenly her world had imploded. The apex of her thighs still ached from Cyn's touch; his seed still dried on her flesh. She wanted him back, yearned to hear him laugh and call her name. But the magic had to end at some point. Even if Henry hadn't destroyed him, she wasn't fool enough to expect her kind lover to last forever.

Letting her head fall to the side, Emma reached down and pinched the skin on the back of her injured hand. The sharp pain prickled. Fresh tears welled to the surface. This was her last chance to see if, maybe, this had all been a wonderful dream, but the weight in her chest was too heavy and the scent of copper and gunpower still permeated the air.

This was real, and her beloved gingerbread man was nothing more than a fragmented avalanche of cookie and icing. "I'm so sorry, Cyn," Emma whispered. "I wish things could have been different . . ."

Suddenly, her promise echoed in her mind.

She would make him anew. She would find a way to bake him back to life.

Using the back of her hand, Emma wiped at the mixture of tears and snot that had collected beneath her nose, then straightened. She gathered as many slabs of gingerbread in her arms as she could and hurried to the kitchen without another glance at her husband's bloodied corpse.

After setting the broken hunks of gingerbread on the counter, Emma grabbed her apron from where it still lay in a crumpled heap, along with the upset bag of flour she'd knocked over when Cyn spun her around and thrust his thick cock inside her. Tying the strands around her waist, she held on to the memory of his touch, his smile.

Emma's eyes continued to burn with tears as she swept the spilled flour into a pan. She could still feel Cyn's hands on her waist, his hot mouth sucking on the swell of her breast. She'd only known him for one afternoon, but in that short time, he'd awoken something so passionate and primal within her that the absence of his presence now burned like a physical brand pressed to her chest.

After washing her hands, Emma poured fresh flour into a large mixing bowl, delighting in the fine particles tickling her lashes.

Oh, sugar. I love watching you get your hands dirty.

Cyn's voice wove through her mind, and phantom heat enveloped her waist as if he were standing right behind her, hands trailing down to stroke her eager pearl. Emma pulled the recipe book down from its nook on the shelf and thumbed to the page she sought. A small hand-drawn gingerbread man illustrated the top right corner. Eagerly, she scrambled around the kitchen, tossing ingredients and measuring spoons onto the counter beside the bowl.

"Soon, Cyn. Soon, I'll bring you back to me."

ACKNOWLEDGEMENTS

This book would not exist without so many people. First to my brilliant editor, Chelsea Cambeis, I am forever indebted to you for the magic you cast, transforming my hodge-podge story into something so dynamic and full. To my cover designer, Neil J Hart, thank you so much for bringing my vision of this stunning cover to life. Molly Likovich, thank you for all your insight and support for this novella, even in the early stages. Bradley Poage, thank you for designing my beautiful website and always being there to lift me up and provide kind words of encouragement. To Samantha Moran, thank you for taking me under your wing and letting me bounce ideas off you. To my amazing beta readers, Kelsey, J.A., and Chey, thank you for reading my drafts, and not only offering constructive feedback, but also excitement at seeing Cyn and Emma's story come to life. A huge thank you to the Booktok community on TikTok, without whom I would never have been inspired to write my own spicy tale. Lastly, to my family. Jack and Joanna, thank you for playing so nicely while Mommy wrote all day and to my husband, Daniel, thank you for baking me the best chocolate chip cookies a baker's wife could ask for.

ABOUT THE AUTHOR

Caytlyn Brooke is an award-winning author of three novels and known for her inability to write a story without including a gruesome character death. As a graduate of UAlbany, she majored in psychology, but it was a Grimm fairytale course that reignited her dream to create her own twisted tales. She lives in the soaring capitol of America with her husband, Daniel, and her children, Jack and Joanna. She also has an orange cat who is not happy about her recent diet. Caytlyn is a terrible baker, but loves to eat gingerbread cookies.